WHAT'S IN THE BOX

WHAT'S IN THE BOX

IF THEY HAD A VOICE

BRAD AYERS

Night Rain Books

Cover Illustration by Allyson Durkin

FIRST EDITION

Printed in the United States of America

ISBN 978-1-7348739-3-1

Night Rain Books / Night Rain Press
PO Box 445
Tillamook, OR 97141

Night.Rain.Press@gmail.com
http://NightRainBooks.com

CONTENTS

INTRODUCTION TO WHAT'S IN THE BOX?

How many boxes have you come in contact within your lifetime? Hard to determine isn't it? Most everything it seems comes in a box, or is put in a box, or is sent in a box. And then there are a jumble of things called boxes or given a name with a box term added like a mailbox, boxcar, or hinted at like the term, "boxed in". And even plants and animals get in on the box name like Boxwood and Box Turtle. I don't know about insects but would not doubt they are in on the box name also.

Seems we are surrounded by box names. You can't avoid this conclusion as you think about boxes. Chances are you and a number of boxes and box terms have met, shared an experience or two, and even said hello or goodbye with emotion. These few stories will start you thinking and wondering how much a box, even a special box, somewhere, sometime, has been a part of your life.

So, explore these stories and see what memories come alive for you.

1

PUT MY FLAG UP

I WAS YOUR TRUSTED MAILBOX IN THE DAY.

A few years ago, my glory days seemed like they were fading. I used to be your main source of news and even junk mail. Then came the Internet with online shopping, electronic bill paying, secure document transmittal, greeting cards, announcements, and banking. The internet even kicked out the once indispensable fax machine. Nothing new here, I guess, as so many technologies over our history have come and gone.

Guess what? My mailbox has survived them all.

Now I am even getting a slight reinvention with all that online shipping stuff you buy going through the mail. Not sure where all this is headed, but who could have guessed ten to twenty years ago where we would be now? All I can say is, don't count us out yet.

I like to remember our glory days. The days when you rushed out to greet the mailman. The mailman would even hand you the mail before it was put in my box. I didn't mind since I was the meeting place for this happy transaction. I brought you and the mail together. I was your trusted mailbox. I even held your mail securely when you were gone a day or two, or during rain showers or snowstorms. I even had a red flag to raise alerting the mailman when you wanted to send a letter. I was a vital two-way meeting place so important during these long-ago days. You kept me up and maintained to clearly mark your home. I was often made with a special design and so proud to be only for you and your mail.

As you think back through all the memories you get a little teary-eyed. So many important and treasured things have passed through my mailbox for you. Yes, there were all the monthly bills and that endless stream of junk mail. You had to put up with all that just so you could get to the real good stuff. Your special magazines, greeting cards, an occasional check, even birthday presents or sympathy cards. Announcements of happy and sad events. A special invitation perhaps tops the list. And in our heyday, I gave you those very personal letters from friends and family. Who is to say what your most important mail was?

So, through all the changes past and future, I will keep my flag up, straight, and tall. We will always be the best friends.

See you when the next mail arrives.

2

CARDBOARD BOX SPOKESPERSON

I DID NOT ASK FOR THIS JOB. I'M JUST an ordinary cardboard box.

But I guess someone, or some box, had to take the lead.

So, hang on, here we go.

I have been around for quite a while. I am probably not the oldest box. But I guess I am fairly popular, as boxes go. And I am probably the best known or the one that comes most to mind when someone says," hand me that box." Maybe that's why my box friends asked me to represent all of the legitimate boxes out there. The true boxes. Not the pretend ones who claim a box attribute but fail when you get right down to it.

Take for example box canyon. How can a canyon that has only three or four of the required six sides be a box? Yes, it really only has two sides, a back that is probably just were the two sides meet, and a floor, claim to be a box? We real six-sided boxes really resent this. It is an insult to our proud heritage. We are the true boxes. Why can't a canyon with a limited entrance and exit be called something else?

Hey, I just said something about heritage you need to think about. What are the origins of a box? Who decided a box had more or less straight sides and square corners? How did all this box stuff start anyway? I can understand the need to put stuff away, but why in a box? And is a box only for keeping stuff from getting away? What about keeping something from getting into it? Whatever, or whoever, boxes certainly caught on and have stayed around for a long time.

Then there are the many things that claim to be a box that are just imposters. They couldn't hold hot air. Even technology has borrowed our name. Like that DropBox computer application, and terms used on forms such as "fill in the box" or even people saying "think outside of the box" for just more creative thinking. You know, this is getting ridiculous. I can't go on. I am afraid I have failed at being a spokesperson. I am going to stop even trying to define what a box is or isn't. I am afraid we have lost all control of our heritage.

We should have filed for a patent or trademark.

Now it's too late.

3

LUNCH BOX, OR BOX LUNCH

L<small>ET'S HAVE LUNCH</small>.

Either way we have two things in common. A box and a lunch.

When you hear my name, a many-experienced image from your past forms quickly. It takes you back to your early school days or even to those work jobs when you were younger. Inside my metal or plastic box is something good to eat. Things you may have been thinking about for what seems like forever as the lunch hour has been so slow to arrive.

Now lunch time is finally here. So, find a good spot at the table, under a tree, on a bench, or just sit on the grass with friends. Open me slowly, one latch at a time. Observe the assorted contents. Take a quick inventory. Is it all there? Any surprises or disappointments? Plan carefully what to eat first, and then plan the rest in sequence. Sounds like this takes a long time but you accomplish it in mere seconds. Check the time again. Now you begin.

There never has been quite such a wonderful lunch box since your first one. Kind of like your first kiss. A six-sided box to be sure. It is therefore a true box. One of the legitimate ones. It has a top, four sides, and a bottom. It securely holds the highlight of your day. As you get into it you discover its real magic. It has held the contents perfectly intact. Even that slight bumping this morning in line or the drop on the school bus did not spoil your lunchtime treats. And every so often, hidden under the napkin, was your mother's note. "Have a good day." Oh yes, an after-school music lesson appointment reminder is sometimes added. The "have a good day" note was nice, but the music lesson note spoiled things a bit.

Fortunately, most of the lunch box memories are pleasant ones. We were real pals. And we transitioned through several designs and versions over the years. The early cartoon ones, the adventure and superheroes, and finally, the last ones that were just rather plain. Function wise they all worked great but when it came time to upgrade as you grew older you and I knew it was time. You could no longer be seen with me. I understood. Every kid goes through it. It is a part of growing up and you had just outgrown me. I stayed behind and got passed on to your younger brother.

I will never forget you.

Your lunch box pal.

4

YOUR KEEPSAKE BOX

I AM USUALLY ON THE SMALL SIDE. A NICE-LOOKING BOX WITH smooth edges. Not that drab-looking cardboard. Or maybe even a carefully crafted wood or metal box.

A neat lid, even hinged, soft, perhaps with felt or flocking, and a nice color.

We keepsake boxes have come in so many forms I can't possibly describe them all. Let's just say we are, each one, precious to you, the owner. And special for not only what we hold, but for the memories we bring back to you. No doubt my keepsake box means a lot. I might have been a unique gift. Maybe there was something in me at a memorable time and place. And, even that long ago loved one in your life could have received or given you something special in me.

I am the box you choose to keep and place all special things in. Most of these are small so that is why our smaller size is so appropriate. I was carefully chosen to be just the right size. Not too wide as to let the contents shift and slide too much. Not so deep things seem to get lonely. And not so small the lid would not close securely. We keepsake boxes are exactly right. You seem to agree each time you look in to find something, or just to remember the past for a few moments.

Oh, the emotions we keepsake boxes inspire as you open us. Only you, opening the lid every now and then, can understand this. Feelings seem to overtake you. No book or computer could store and describe it all. One at a time you pick up and hold each of the contents carefully in your hand. Turn each one over, some get a close up look, and are grasped tighter before being returned to the box. Then another item catches your memory, and you pick it up and repeat the cycle of remembering. You sometimes add to the box , but for some unexplained reason things today seem less special as do the contents long ago placed in the box.

You enjoy telling the younger ones sitting next to you about why these things are in the box. You seem to be forgetting just a little bit each time you look but you can't forget the emotion, and it sweeps over you again. You try to explain, but the words seem locked away.

You relish this time, but know it is special and reserved for just an occasional visit. Look too often and it would spoil things. The treasure of these times must be kept.

As you replace my lid, I whisper comfort to you. I will always be your keepsake box.

5

CUSTOM LOGO BOX

ARE THERE ANY OTHER KINDS THESE days?

My name and distinctive logo cannot be mistaken. I have made my mark on the world of boxes. I am speaking for all the great custom logo boxes of the world. Each one trying hard to be king of the box world.

But I am savvy enough to know trends, products, trademarks, and most other marketing images never last. They get revised, updated, so-called improved on, some even have their own marketing campaigns, and some are replaced or just plain discontinued after all the promotion. So, I will enjoy seeing you recognize me, telling others about me, and basking in the fame while it lasts. I will make as much out of it as possible until my fate is certain.

Wait just a minute!

I guess you did not realize I had opinions about how I am treated. If I am such a famous box, a regular household name so to speak, why am I used for the cat litter and dirty rags, or just thrown out with the trash? Some of you responsibility take the recycle route but even then my proud logo is buried with all those only plain boxes. I get stuffed and squeezed in some big dumpster and then carted off to an uncertain ending. I would rather not say any more. It's too depressing. The wannabe king of boxes treated as a common ordinary cardboard box. Yuk.

All of us custom logo boxes are trying to keep our prime image and hard-fought position in the box world. By all accounts we are making some progress. Our numbers keep multiplying. I just hope we have enough ink. Hey, I just said "prime" a few sentences back. Did that ring any bells for you? Is my box then also synonymous with something free? Now wait another minute. How can I hope to be the king of boxes and have a free image? Shouldn't I command a higher status? I should be expensive, not free. What marketing guy made that image mistake?

Yes, it's true. Even we custom logo boxes have problems. What a hard life we live—short as it is sometimes. I know some friends of mine who only got used for one customer shipment. Then off to the trash they were sent.

There just has to be something wrong here.

6

TOOLBOX MEMORIES

NOW A TOOLBOX IS SOMETHING EVERYONE HAS, OR HAS HEARD OF, or known someone who had one, or had one dropped on your toe. That last one was in case you were not paying attention.

We are talking about toolboxes here! Pay attention, focus.

My guess is, based on how I have been treated, toolboxes have had a particularly rough time of it. We are tough. We can take a lot of punishment. We tend to last a long time, even passed down through several generations. That goes for the tools inside also. We have protected them like they were our family. Some tools we hold are rare antiques of some early craftsmen who knew the value of protecting and caring for them. Some of us are from fathers or uncles, friends, and next-door neighbors. And some were orphaned along the path of use and reacquired at a garage sale.

But I kind of rushed over my description of toolbox contents by just talking about tools. I am much more important than just a tool carrier. I have been known to keep a wide array of things. Some so strange you can't remember what they were used for. And then, every tenth toolbox or so gets used for something having absolutely nothing to do with tools. I guess we look secure and a good place for valuables or important papers. Treasured photos have been known to hide in our boxes. Maybe we get sat on or used as a step up. Some of us have held dangerous contents like guns and knives. Then there is the deep and dark stuff too scary to talk about. And that is only the start of what we could discuss.

Let's skip ahead to our future.

I honestly don't see any stopping us. Our future looks bright. New materials, colors, styles, custom uses, and that must-have appeal. Some of us older ones will get replaced. No doubt about it. We served our time, did our job, and now we make way for the younger generation.

I always thought we were timeless, but such is not the case.

We rust a bit, loose that new sheen, and fall by the wayside to the latest toolbox design on some endcap promotion in the home improvement store.

But there will always be a toolbox in your garage, shed, or household.

7

SPORT BOXES

No story about boxes would be complete without including the role we play in sports. I know you will think us six-sided real boxes are getting carried away but just come along and let your funny side have a laugh.

Let's start with baseball. How many boxes are there in baseball? Start counting. "Batter's box", "box score", "bandbox", "crackerbox"," hot box", "thru the box", "knocked out of the box", first and third base "coach's boxes", and "Trading Card boxes" to name a few. Now consider the batter's box expressions like "step in the box," "dive out of the box" "hit in the box," "back in the box," and you get the idea boxes are a key part of the National Pastime.

But baseball cannot claim to have exclusive rights to box expressions. What about the "service box" in tennis, "penalty box" in hockey, or "boxed out" in basketball, "in the box" used in soccer and football, or "tee box" used in golf, along with "press box" used in most all sports. But this is only the start with the major sports. We have invaded almost all of the sports world so far. To stretch a bit, let us include sandboxes where sports in some small form have been known to take place from an early age. I will leave the rest to your curiosity, imagination, or even a memory.

So, what do we have to say about all this box terminology? The real boxes are divided on this. There are the traditionalists who hold to the true definition. A strict interpretation of the six-sided enclosure. But a growing movement thinks any use of the term box should be welcomed and even encouraged. This more liberal attitude seems to be winning on this if you look at today's language use. Box terms are actually rampant (excuse my exaggeration) in the conversation. The one common link seems to imply some kind of confinement or constraint, or the lack there of. Other than that, it is wide open to describe just about any aspect of society, including our actions, and feelings like, "I feel boxed in," or "don't put me in that box."

Have we covered the subject?

Can we agree that boxes of all kinds have a bright future?

Good.

8

PLAY BOXES

THERE ARE BOXES FOR A LOT OF THINGS BUT WHO EVER THOUGHT boxes were for playing?

Yes, everything from the make-a-fort types to Halloween costumes. Even school science projects get in on the fun with pin hole experiments and solar lights. When you think about it, boxes are fun. I bet you had more than one in your time.

Typically, this story starts with an arrival like a dryer or washing machine similar to my case. Although I could have just as easy been holding a smaller appliance or piece of furniture. After unpacking, I was put to the side in the garage while the adults attended to the instillation of its contents.

Then it happened. The kids discovered me and then went running to dad.

"Hey dad, can we have the box?"

My story is repeated over and over so many times it makes me dizzy. So, let me now take you through how things play out.

Slightly distracted, the dad says to the kid's question, "sure," not realizing what has just been set in motion. A whole bunch of imagination, that's what. And along the way, as the transformation takes place, dad and mom both can't resist and get in on the fun with suggested graphics for decoration, a door here, or window there. They get a renewal of their youth from remembering back to when they got their first play box.

It's a fort, a castle, or race car!

Then the play starts with all sorts of games and pretend things. The fun takes over the house, garage or even moved out to the backyard. The box does it's best to hold up but eventually a jump, then a hole, a rip, a tear, and finally the collapse ends the play box. If lucky, it has lasted several days when the end comes. By that time all that is left are the memories. And those memories will last a lifetime until they come around again with another "Hey dad, can I have the box?"

But you know what? The box actually enjoyed it all. I know I did. The ending to my life as box was quite a surprise, however. No one told me at the factory this was coming. I thought I had done my job on delivery. They told me to protect my contents, stay neat and tidy, and in a day or two after delivery I would smoothly go out with the next trash or recycle pickup. So, imagine the surprise when all these little kids started crawling inside me and making some kind of vehicle, or spooky castle, a pretend house, a fort, or hideout. All out of me. I heard a lot of whispering and planning. Most of it was fast and with giggling and laughing. But I caught the spirit of the fun and tried my best to be the best play box ever.

You can learn from us boxes.

We all have jobs to do, yes, even a box. But there are two sides to look at.

The most rewarding part of life is giving fun to others.

9

_____

A SHOE BOX LIFE

I WAS A SHOE BOX.

Most of us are about the size to comfortably hold a pair of shoes. While some are plain, others have colorful designs. Many have brand names, models, and numbers to identify sizes and styles. Records show a shoe box became the mode of storage, shipment, and display for new shoes in the mid-1800s as shoes transitioned from a cobbler shop industry to manufacturing and retail store sales.

There is quite an interesting history of post-sale shoe box uses including everything you can imagine needing low-cost temporary or even longer-term safe keeping. Holding and storing old pictures and letters and cards is a common use along with an endless variety of others. Most shoe boxes and their contents are stored on the closet shelf, under the bed, or any flat surface.

But while this is interesting history it is not why I am telling you this story. More specifically it is about one particular shoe box story. A story of total commitment. It is my story.

After holding a pair of women's shoes in a mall store for what seemed like forever I was finally sold one day and went to live in a nice home. A suburban home with a dog, a young boy, the mother, and father. The shoes I had once held were now being worn daily by mother during household chores, grocery shopping, and the ordinary activities of the day. I was surprised when I did not go directly to the trash. Perhaps because I was sturdy, and a good size for some things I soon found out were on the way? So, I was put on a shelf and saved for what would become a very special purpose.

As it turned out my arrival was only a few days before Poncho's. Poncho was a blue parakeet who would quickly become mother's favorite pet. Not just today, but any day in her life she would remind all of us. And Poncho seemed to know it. Remember, I was just a silent shoe box observer but even I could see this relationship developing into something special. Poncho had the run of the house and would fly to mother's outstretched finger, then repeatedly chirp what we were told were actual words. No one else could make this out but mother said Poncho was learning words. She was sure of it.

Life went on for over two years with Poncho being the center of household entertainment and me holding the growing contents of snapshot pictures with Poncho and mother, a few small bird toys, a "How to Train Parakeets" pamphlet, and a newspaper article about birds as pets. Both Poncho and I were a team. We were so lucky.

I must say, being a shoe box was better than I ever anticipated. I was told at the factory my life would be over when the shoes were sold. But things were turning out quite different. I was given a special place just right for my size and shape. I was at rest most of the time, but always doing a good job holding something special, something important. When I was taken down from the shelf I was handled carefully, most tenderly you would say, as my contents were reviewed and occasionally added to. Then I would be replaced, just as easy as I had come out, sliding back into my resting space. Yes, my shoe box life was wonderful.

But then the story takes a turn.

One day Poncho started to slow down flying around the house. He stopped chirping too. No more mister entertainment. With tears flowing down redden cheeks, mother held him, talked softly, and tried to cheer him up. But nothing was working. That's when I was called into action.

A shoe box has to be ready, and I was.

My contents were unloaded, and Poncho was placed inside me on a soft cloth. The kitchen oven was turned on low, and with door open, Poncho and I were placed on the open door for warmth. Mother kept a constant vigil for two days and nights. Slowly Poncho started to move a little. Then a weak chirp was heard and finally more movement. Gradually Poncho regained his health, and within a few days recovered to again fly around the house, and chirp what mother told everyone were actual words.

Poncho went on to have a long and loved life for a parakeet and I was again returned to be the keeper of all things Poncho. In reflection, I think my holding Poncho on the oven door was my most important contribution.

Who ever thought a shoe box could have such an important life?

AFTERWORD: IF THEY HAD A VOICE

Have you ever wondered what our world has to say?

We go about our lives midst all forms of non-human objects with only a passing thought, or no thought at all about them. And rarely have we even attempted a conversation.

What if we listen closely? What would they tell us? What could we learn?

You might be surprised at just how much they have to say about us.

This series of short stories started by an impromptu response to a prompt given in a writing class I took. The prompt was to write for 14 minutes on "something you keep." Out of the blue the image of a beach rock in my hand came to mind. Probably from one of many walks on the beach at Cape Meares, and even seeing others looking for that special rock. Or even seeing someone's beach and shell collection neatly arranged or scattered around. We all have picked up a beach rock, held it a while, and maybe kept it to go home or dropped it for another. That day I wrote about this experience, completed the assignment, and filed it away with that hint of something undone.

Several months later as I was typing my handwritten responses to past writing prompts into the computer, I again read the story I had titled, "The Hopeful Beach Rock." I lingered a while, reading it again several times. And for some mysterious reason the stories started coming one after the other about other beach objects like driftwood, waves, the ocean breeze, and more. All had something to say about us. They even ask questions and heard our thoughts. They started our memories working and recalling earlier times, ones that were happy, sad, and adventurous.

After doing several beach stories I started to get images of other things we pass by, touch, or work with that should also get a chance to talk. Thus, started a much larger series of stories including things we sit on, doors we go through, and a range of others you will want to read about in the Voices collections.

This is the best part. I realized that in telling these as short stories, some call flash fiction, I could give you the chance to make it your own. I give each a range of emotions and experiences, but you will find it compelling to fill in and expand with your own.

As you read the stories remember only the non-human object does the talking. You have only to listen. The chair, for example, will ask you to remember what you were doing and thinking as you sat for a while, then suggests answers and asks even more questions. The door will recall memories of your emotions the door had observed as you passed through. Like a mirror, the door reflects these and suggests what you were thinking and whether you had any regrets. The beach rock wonders and asks you if you will keep it or discard it and choose another leaving you to determine the outcome. Interesting life lessons for sure.

Each reader of these stories will have a unique reaction to the observations and answers to the questions because all have different experiences. The one common link is we all have these kinds of memories. And each subsequent reading will only add to the recall and variations, with even new themes and outcomes of your own.

Some stories were written on the lighter side of things, playful, and happy times. Some are more serious with only hints of deeper concerns, but none are scary or tragic. Some have a moral bent and others suggest you read between the lines to get the nuance.

Most stories, however, are just plain fun.

ABOUT THE AUTHOR

I give most of the inspiration credit to the wonderful Northwest and Oregon coast. I arrived in 2015 and have not stopped creating in new and unusual ways. It inspires all art forms, and frankly just about anything you want to do. So, I give thanks for a second chance to prosper including my efforts of fiction writing and just recently song writing.

After a first degree in Fine Arts from California State University I went into business for my professional life. An MBA from the University of Denver followed while working for three major US companies, then running and starting my own along the way.

Concurrent to the business side I was an adjunct professor in the MBA program for the University of Phoenix for over 30 years.

I guess I was destined to return to the creative side of life, now at the ripe old age of 81. Old dogs, new tricks? Perhaps in this case. Yes, this is not your typical "about the author?" Blame the weather.

VOICES PUBLICATION COLLECTION

Beach Voices

Doors We Walk Through

The Chair Has Something To Say

Walk In My Garden

What's In The Box?

Clothes Get Testy

Food Talks Back

ALSO BY BRAD AYERS

A Life's Journey

Beach Voices

The Chair Has Something to Say

Walk in My Garden

www.ingramcontent.com/pod-product-compliance
Lightning Source LLC
Chambersburg PA
CBHW070652130626
46555CB00006B/2843